Urso Brunov

AND THE WHITE EMPEROR

For Hannah & Anthony Owen Jacques from Granddad.
—B.J.

For my mother.
—A.N.

Urso Brunov
AND THE WHITE EMPEROR

BRIAN JACQUES

illustrations by **Alexi Natchev**

PHILOMEL BOOKS

igh up on the roof of the world, Winter spread its cold white cloak. Deep in the forest, Urso Brunov and his tiny bears lay sleeping, snug and warm in their den. Every now and then, there was a small draft from the knotholes in the worn old door. The Brunov home was a big hollow tree. Urso was always promising himself to repair the door and forgetting to do it.

Did I not tell you that Urso Brunov is the Little Father of All Bears? Well, that is his title. He is mighty in battle, strong as an elephant, fierce as a lion and wise as the wisest old owl of the forests. He is also kind, gentle, and a champion defender of all creatures, particularly young ones. He is a Brunov Bear, which means that he stands no taller than your very own thumb.

Be still now and I will tell you a tale of Urso Brunov, the Little Father of All Bears.

Urso Brunov's fine bugle was hanging just inside the door when the wind rushed around the forest, through a knothole in the door, and blew upon it.

Taratataaaaah!

It woke a tiny bear, who became frightened.

"Father, your bugle is playing on its own!"

Urso arose and stroked her head fondly.

"It is only the wind, little Ursulina. Go to sleep, I will attend to it."

He went outdoors into the forest, calling, "Old Uncle Wind, why do you disturb our winter rest?"

The kind Silvery Moon Lady answered him softly from afar. "Little Father, wolves are on the prowl and there are two lost bears at the edge of your forest. Follow Uncle Wind, he will take you there. I will light the way for you, hurry!"

Urso Brunov dressed quickly in his warmest clothes. Then he took his bugle and sped off through the snow, with the wind guiding him and the Silvery Moon Lady lighting his way. So determined was he to rescue the lost bears that he did not notice his own little bears following behind.

Soon he began to hear the baying of hungry wolves ahead.
"*Howoooooooh!*"
"Little Father, hurry, I beg you," sighed Old Uncle Wind. Then
Urso ran very fast indeed. As did his little bears.

Sliding down a long hill, he zoomed out of the forest and came upon a fearsome sight. A young polar bear and her baby brother were out on the plains, surrounded by a pack of large gray wolves.

Swizz! Urso Brunov slid right through the wolves' legs, right into the middle of the awful scene. He cracked the long tassel on his hat top like a whip.

Snap! Crack! Whack!

The wolves drew back, their red tongues lolling out hungrily and their sharp teeth bared. Urso Brunov blew a blast on his bugle and roared, "You are scaring these poor young bears! Stop this snarling or you'll be sorry. I am Urso Brunov!"

The wolves fell silent, all save one, who was the leader. He snarled nastily, louder than ever.

Urso did not like disobedient wolves. With a powerful leap he landed on the leader's head. Then he blew several mighty bugle blasts into the wolf's ears.

Barratatatah! Barratatatah! Barrrraaaaaaah!

The fierce wolf collapsed, wailing pitifully.

"Stop, stop, Little Father, you are bursting my eardrums!"

Urso waved his bugle threateningly. "I will blow your ears off if you do not take your pack out of my sight!"

The wolf pack fled like gray dawn shadows.

Urso spoke gently to the older polar bear. "Do not be afraid of Urso Brunov, I have come to help you."

The pretty young polar bear wiped away an icy tear. "I am Princess Arctura, and this is my baby brother, Prince Bublo. The Great White Emperor Balanco and the Empress Tiralina are our parents. We come from the Land of Rainbow Lights, far across the deep sea. I was walking Bublo along the coast there when the ice broke away. We were swept out to sea on a piece of it. We have not seen our home for many, many days. I fear we are lost forever!"

The tiny bears, who had been hiding and watching, gasped aloud at this. Urso Brunov heard them and turned around.

"Well, my own lost bears. You should be home, asleep like all good tiny bears." They were afraid their father would be angry with them, but instead Urso smiled. "No matter. When creatures are in danger, we all must help. Tonight you young ones will come with me."

The princess polar bear began weeping sadly, for she was still frightened.

"Dry your eyes, young one. I promise I will take you and your brother home to the Land of Rainbow Lights. And I must tell you that the Little Father of All Bears always keeps his promises. So don't be sad."

The princess smiled charmingly, and baby Bublo gurgled happily.

"But first," Urso told them, "I must gather gifts we might need along the way."

And so Urso, who was as smart as he was brave, collected baskets of berries and nuts, and the five bears, two large and three small, set off for the Land of Rainbow Lights.

When they reached the edge of the forest, Princess Arctura saw the snow, wide and deep over the flatlands. She covered her face in dismay. "Oh, dearie me, we will never be able to get through. What shall we do?"

"Fear not, little one, I will solve this problem. For am I not Urso Brunov?" He blew his bugle loud and clear. *Taraaah! Tataraaaah!*

There was a mighty rumble of trotters and a whirling cloud of powdery snow. It was a whole herd of wild boar, with curving tusks, fierce red eyes and rough bristly hides. They surrounded the travelers, causing them much alarm, but the brave Urso Brunov just laughed aloud. "Meet my friend Snurff and her herd—they will not harm you. Ho there, Snurff, you old acorn cruncher. Would you like to earn a fine basket of nuts?"

Snurff gave a snorty chuckle. "I will do anything for a whole basket of nuts. What is your wish, Little Father?"

Urso Brunov pointed to the snowbound flatlands. "I need to take these two young polar bears to their home. Can you make a path through this deep snow to the sea for us, my friend?"

Snurff gave an extra-snorty chuckle. "O Urso Brunov, consider it done. Let us go to the sea, my boars. Charge!"

The boar herd thundered off over the flatlands. Behind them they left a smooth path, trampled flat under their pounding trotters.

Urso Brunov took up his bugle again.

"Good old Snurff! Now we need strong creatures to carry us along gently. Riding on rough, bristly boars would be too bumpy for princes, princesses, and Brunovs." He blew one long, sweet trill. *Tataaaaaaaaaah!*

Two beautiful deer emerged from the forest. Urso smiled. "These are my friends Hamul, Chieftain of Stags, and his lovely wife, Sorelva. They will carry us safely to the deep sea."

Hamul lowered his large, spreading antlers. "The Little Father has helped us many times. It will be an honor to carry you to the deep sea. Climb on our backs and make yourselves comfortable."

The bears clambered up on both deer. In a moment they were bounding like the wind along the path made by Snurff's boar herd.

Urso stood up on top of Hamul's high antlers and started singing.
For such a tiny bear he had a huge, strong bass voice.
"Hiyah! Hoyoh! We cross these lands so wide.
Hoyoh! Hiyah! What's on the other side?
That deep blue sea where fishes play
and big ice mountains float, they say,
with Urso Brunov come away. Hiyaaaaaaah!"

For a day, a night, and another day they traveled. Never once did Hamul or Sorelva stop or stumble. When they arrived on the thick ice ledges of the coast, Snurff and her boars were waiting to greet them. Urso Brunov gave Snurff two baskets of nuts, for he knew how greedy boars could be. Thanking the deer warmly, Urso gave them baskets of plump, juicy berries.

Princess Arctura stared in awe at the deep sea. Once more she covered her face and started to weep. "Dearie me, this sea is so deep and wide! It will be impossible to cross it. What are we to do?"

"Do not worry. I will get us across the sea, for am I not Urso Brunov?"

Taking his bugle, Urso dipped his head under the sea. It was icy cold, but he was the bravest of bears. With his head beneath the water, he blew some bubbly notes. *Bloggletaraaah-glockle-ockle!*

Then something rather strange began happening.

A dark, shiny hump appeared out of the deep sea. It began rising, higher and higher and still yet higher, until it almost blocked out the sky. It was truly humongous. Princess Arctura stared up at the big, dark mountain. "Little Father, what is it?"

The mountain blinked, and the princess and her brother found themselves gazing into a giant eye. Urso shook water out of his bugle.

"This is Rumool, King of Whales and Oceans. We are old friends, I am sure he will help us."

King Rumool smiled. "Urso Brunov, my little friend, what can I do for you?" His voice was mild and calm as a meadow breeze.

"I must take these young white bears to their home, the Land of Rainbow Lights," Urso answered.

King Rumool winked at the prince and princess. "They look so pretty and well mannered, how could I refuse?" King Rumool swam off, farther up the coast. He raised his colossal tail flukes and brought them down hard on the ice ledge. *Craaaaaack!* A broad, flat chunk broke off. Setting his powerful head against it, the whale pushed it back to the travelers. "Here is your boat—get on board and I will take you back to your home!"

When the bears were safely on the ice boat, Urso Brunov leapt lightly onto King Rumool's head and blew his bugle. *Tata-tatatata-taaaaah!*

Off they sailed into the deep blue sea, with the whale pushing their craft along. The tiny Brunov bears sang joyfully.

"Have no worries, have no cares,
Urso Brunov is the one!
Little Father of All Bears,
he will always get things done!
Greatly loved by one and all,
every creature good and true,
when they hear his bugle call,
sun and moon and old wind too,
they will answer his request.
Urso Brunov they love best!"

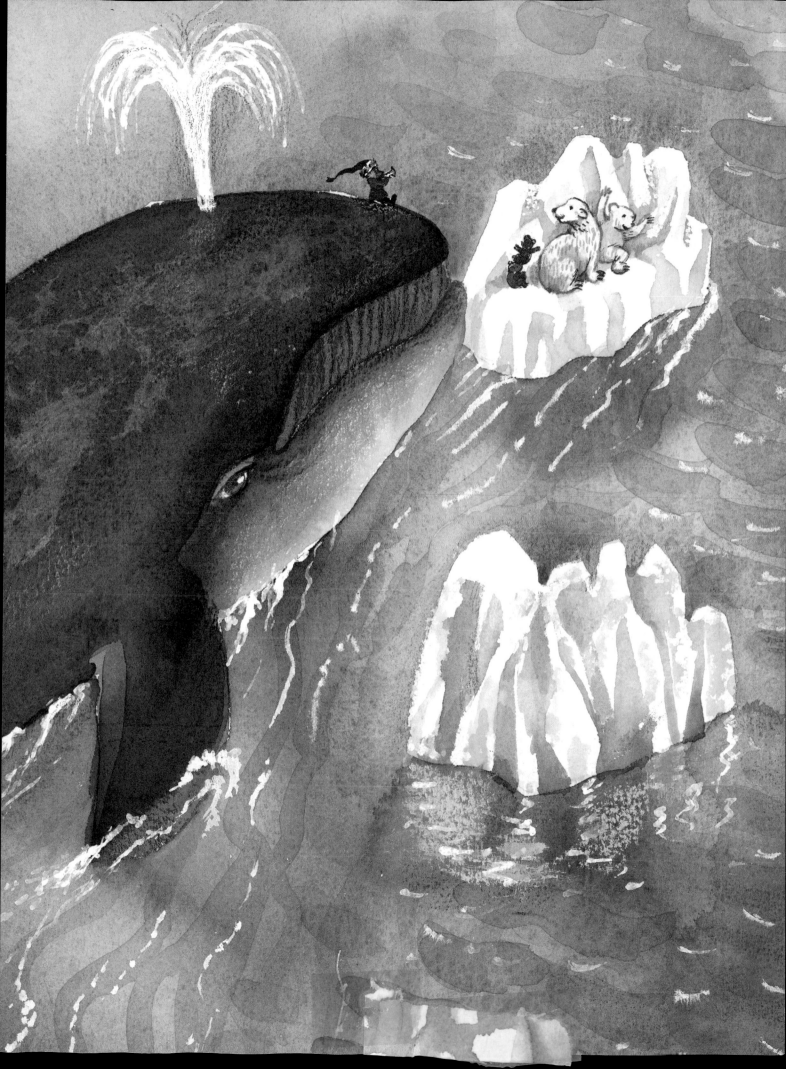

They sailed the deep sea for two days and two silent star-scattered nights. Just before dawn on the second night, Urso Brunov cried out to Rumool, "Spout water high, my friend, I feel our journey is almost done!"

The mighty whale sent up a whooshing jet of steam and water from the blowhole in his head. Urso Brunov went up with it. "Land ho!" he cried, and blew his bugle.

Princess Arctura lifted baby Bublo up. "Look, little brother, there are the Rainbow Lights. We are almost home!"

Many creatures were waiting onshore to meet them. Black bears, brown bears, polar bears, walruses and seals. The travelers were put on a wonderful snow sleigh, which was drawn by a reindeer. Off they went amid jingling sleigh bells, up a high hill to a vast ice dome. The Rainbow Lights shone through its walls, a brilliant riot of color.

The young bears' mother, Empress Tiralina, was overjoyed to see Arctura and Bublo safe and well. As the empress hugged and kissed them, the princess introduced her guests.

"Mother, these tiny bears are my dear friends the Brunovs. They saved us from the wolves and journeyed far to bring us home to you."

Urso Brunov bowed politely. "I also brought you gifts of fruit, nuts and berries from my forest."

Suddenly, the White Emperor Balanco entered the dome. He greeted his young bears fondly and had a quiet word with the empress before turning to Urso Brunov.

Every creature fell silent as the emperor stared down at his very small guest.

"So, you are Urso Brunov. I did not think you would be so tiny, if you'll pardon my mentioning it."

Urso Brunov laughed aloud. "And you are the White Emperor Balanco. I did not think you would be so large, if you'll pardon my mentioning it."

Every beast gasped at the mighty emperor being addressed in such a fashion by the tiny bear.

Then the emperor threw back his head and laughed.

And the empress laughed, too.

Soon every bear of every size was laughing. The ice dome echoed with merriment.

"Urso Brunov, you have brought happiness back to our home!" said the emperor. "Let there be a special celebration! It will be in honor of the Little Father, Urso Brunov, our new friend. We will dance. We will play. We will sing. And we will feast."

The Rainbow Lights flared up in a wonderful dance of weaving colors. Urso Brunov played a loud joyous tune on his bugle as he danced. Everyone danced with him, and oh, how they danced!

For three days and three nights the special celebration continued. They sang the funniest songs, danced the wildest dances, played the merriest games and feasted on the emperor's finest food and drink.

And all that time the most beautiful sound on Earth filled the vast ice dome. The sound of laughter!

When the time came for Urso Brunov to depart, the kindly empress invited him to return every winter and repeat the festivities. Urso gallantly bowed and kissed her paw.

"You have my thanks, and my promise I will return. For am I not Urso Brunov, the Little Father who always keeps his promises!"

The Great White Emperor hung a huge square medal of solid gold around the tiny bear's neck. He bowed to Urso Brunov. "I had this medal made specially for you, my good friend. May Old Uncle Wind and these good birds speed you safely back to your home. Good-bye."

Three plump geese waddled into the ice dome. Their leader saluted with his wing. "I have been sent by the Silvery Moon Lady to carry you back home to the far forests."

Urso smiled. "Thank you, friend. My Brunov Bears need their winter rest."

The tiny bears mounted the soft, feathery backs of the geese, which were very comfortable, and were fast asleep even before they got off the ground.

Away the beautiful geese soared, like boats with sails outspread. As they reached the deep sea, Urso looked back to see all the bears standing outside the ice dome, waving. In the waters below, Rumool the Whale King sent up a tall jet of steam and spray as a farewell. Silvery Moon Lady saw them passing through her silent acres of star-dusted sky. She did not speak for fear of waking the tiny bears. On the far coast, Snurff and her boar herd were asleep, snoring and grunting. They did not wake, but lay there dreaming of baskets loaded with nuts, as most boars do. Hamul, Chieftain of Stags, and his lovely wife, Sorelva, each opened one eye when the geese flew over the forest edge. They went back to their sleep satisfied that Urso Brunov and his tiny bears had returned to the roof of the world.

When they arrived at the hollow tree, Urso Brunov thanked the geese and gave them berries from his larder. Then, taking care to be extra quiet, he carried his tiny bears inside to their hammocks. The Little Father gave a long yawn and was about to go to his own bed when he remembered something he had promised himself.

Going outside, Urso found the emperor's big, square gold medal where he had left it. Now, I don't know whether you are aware that Urso Brunov was also the world's greatest fix-it bear. It did not take him long to remove the old front door of his hollow-tree home. He replaced it with the big, square gold medal, which fit perfectly. He dusted off his paws, murmuring, "I remember promising myself to do something about that door, and Urso Brunov always keeps his promises!"

PHILOMEL BOOKS
A division of Penguin Young Readers Group.
Published by The Penguin Group.
Penguin Group (USA) Inc., 375 Hudson Street, New York, NY 10014, U.S.A.
Penguin Group (Canada), 90 Eglinton Avenue East, Suite 700, Toronto, Ontario M4P 2Y3, Canada
(a division of Pearson Penguin Canada Inc.).
Penguin Books Ltd, 80 Strand, London WC2R 0RL, England.
Penguin Ireland, 25 St. Stephen's Green, Dublin 2, Ireland (a division of Penguin Books Ltd).
Penguin Group (Australia), 250 Camberwell Road, Camberwell, Victoria 3124, Australia
(a division of Pearson Australia Group Pty Ltd).
Penguin Books India Pvt Ltd, 11 Community Centre, Panchsheel Park, New Delhi - 110 017, India.
Penguin Group (NZ), 67 Apollo Drive, Rosedale, North Shore 0632, New Zealand
(a division of Pearson New Zealand Ltd).
Penguin Books (South Africa) (Pty) Ltd, 24 Sturdee Avenue, Rosebank, Johannesburg 2196, South Africa.
Penguin Books Ltd, Registered Offices: 80 Strand, London WC2R 0RL, England.

Design by Semadar Megged.   Text set in 14-point Caslon 3.   The art was done in watercolor.

Library of Congress Cataloging-in-Publication Data
Jacques, Brian.   Urso Brunov and the White Emperor / Brian Jacques ; illustrated by Alexi Natchev.
p. cm.   Summary: Urso Brunov, the Little Father of All Bears, who stands no bigger than your thumb and
always keeps his promises, saves two lost polar bears with the help of some of his friends.
[1. Fairy tales. 2. Bears—Fiction. 3. Animals—Fiction. 4. Winter—Fiction.] I. Natchev, Alexi, ill. II. Title.
PZ8.J197Ur 2008   [E]—dc22   2008000659
ISBN 978-0-399-23792-8
10 9 8 7 6 5 4 3 2 1